Also by Sheryl Berk and Carrie Berk

The Cupcake Club Series
Peace, Love, and Cupcakes
Recipe for Trouble
Winner Bakes All
Icing on the Cake
Baby Cakes
Royal Icing
Sugar and Spice

Fashion Academy Series
Fashion Academy

Sweet Victory

The Cupcake Club

Sheryl Berk and Carrie Berk

sourcebooks
jabberwocky

Published by Sourcebooks Jabberwocky, an imprint of Sourcebooks, Inc.
P.O. Box 4410, Naperville, Illinois 60567–4410
(630) 961–3900
Fax: (630) 961–2168
www.sourcebooks.com

Library of Congress Cataloging-in-Publication data is on file with the publisher.

Source of Production: Versa Press, East Peoria, Illinois, USA
Date of Production: August 2015
Run Number: 5004594

Printed and bound in the United States of America.
VP 10 9 8 7 6 5 4 3 2 1

In loving memory of Elizabeth Maria Walsh:

You will always be our Luchadora

Up, Up, and Away

Sadie Harris zipped down Frisbee Street on her new RipStik board, imagining herself carving down a powdery white ski slope.

"Yes!" she cheered as she took each curb expertly. She came to a screeching halt at Kylie Carson's house and waved to her friend. Thanks to her new speedy means of transportation—a Christmas gift from her two older brothers—she was the first to arrive at the cupcake club meeting.

"Does that thing only have two wheels?" Kylie gasped. "Sadie, you are a maniac!"

"It's so cool!" Sadie said, picking up the bright-red caster board and flipping it upside down to show Kylie its design. "I can do all these sick tricks—even a three-sixty turn. It's like a snowboard on wheels!"

Kylie nodded. "Yeah, I almost broke my neck on the bunny slope when my parents took me skiing last year.

Better keep me far away from anything that goes fast and downhill."

Sadie smiled. "I could teach you sometime. It's really not hard."

"Not hard for you," Kylie replied. "You ace every sport you try. My parents nicknamed me 'Kylie Klutzarina' when I was three for a reason."

"It has a nice ring to it," Sadie teased her friend. She gave Kylie a playful punch in the arm.

"Since you're so sporty, you're gonna love our latest order," Kylie said. "It's pretty over the top."

No cupcake order could surprise Sadie anymore. Peace, Love, and Cupcakes had created cupcakes for an Elvis impersonator; cupcakes decorated to look like raw sushi; and even cupcakes for dogs, cats, and horses to eat.

"Go ahead—spill," Sadie said. "What's the new order, and are we renaming the club Peace, Love, and Crazy to Bake This?"

"I think we should wait till the rest of the girls get here," Kylie said, stalling her. "But I will give you one little hint: you'll be jumping up and down when I tell you what it is."

☆ ☮ ☆

By the time Jenna Medina, Lexi Poole, and Delaney Noonan—the remaining members of PLC—arrived, Kylie had laid out all the details on her kitchen counter. "So the delivery is Saturday morning, which gives us a week," she said, glancing at the order form. "And the order is for four dozen in two different flavors—something chocolate, something vanilla." She opened her recipe binder and started flipping through it.

"It doesn't sound so complicated." Lexi weighed in. "Sadie told us you said this order was over the top."

"Well, the customer is leaving the design *up* to us, and the sky's the limit," Kylie replied.

Jenna realized her friend was trying to be punny. "There is no way I am delivering these cupcakes jumping out of a plane!"

"Relax! No skydiving." Kylie chuckled. "But you're right about the 'up in the air' part."

"Is this a cupcake order for birds?" Lexi guessed. "'Cause feathers and fondant don't exactly go well together."

"Nope, no birds," Kylie said. "And no helicopters or bungee jumping either."

Jenna scratched her head. "*Qué pasa, chica?* What are you not telling us?"

"The order is for a trampoline birthday party!" Kylie finally revealed. "How much fun is that?"

"Please tell me we don't have to make cupcakes that bounce," Jenna said, groaning.

"Can we do that?" Delaney asked excitedly. She loved to kid around, but she could also be a little clueless sometimes.

"The birthday boy is turning five and has invited his whole kindergarten class to Up, Up, and Away Trampoline Center in Stamford."

"Cool!" Sadie said. "So we have to come up with cupcakes that have a trampoline theme."

"Exactly," Kylie said. "Any ideas?"

For a few minutes, the room was silent as the girls thought hard.

"Feet!" Lexi suddenly tossed out. "Or maybe socks? Isn't that what you wear to jump on a trampoline?"

"Flies," Sadie added. "They're always in the air. And little boys love bugs, right?"

"Falling," Jenna grumped. "As in splat on your face or butt. Which is what I would do on a trampoline."

"Um, I'm not seeing any of those things on a cupcake," Kylie tried her hardest to envision their suggestions, but all she could see was Jenna flopping on a trampoline face-first. As cupcake club president, Kylie had the power to veto an idea—and smelly feet and flies didn't sound particularly appetizing.

"What about balloons—balloons go *up, up, and away* if you accidentally let them go," Delaney suggested. "And they're pretty and colorful—and every birthday party has them."

"That's just it," Sadie jumped in. "Cupcakes with balloons on them are so ordinary. We're PLC. We can do better than that."

Lexi took out her sketchbook. Designing cupcake decorations was her job. "Sadie's right. What if we did something like this…" She drew a cupcake with blue piping around the edges and a black fondant top to represent the trampoline. In the middle of the cupcake was a small figure of a boy bending his knees with his arms in the air.

"Ooh, that is amazing," Kylie said, watching as Lexi used her colored pencils to bring the cupcake to life on the page. "We could use fondant to mold the little jumping guys."

"And no boring vanilla or chocolate flavors either," Jenna insisted. As the official taste tester, it was her job to make each cupcake delectable. "I'm thinking chocolate-chocolate chip cake filled with marshmallow and churro cupcakes with a hint of cinnamon to give the vanilla a kick."

"Nice." Sadie high-fived her. "Do you suppose we'll get to try out those trampolines when we make the delivery?"

"*Tu mejor que yo*—better you than me!" Jenna said. "I get motion sickness if my little brothers bounce on the couch."

"Then I'd say we have a plan," Kylie said, taking notes in her binder. "Let's get jumpin' on those cupcake recipes."

Anything You Can Do, I Can Do...

Saturday morning, bright and early, Sadie's dad showed up with Sadie in his contractor's truck to drive with Kylie to the trampoline party.

"This sounds like an easy order," Mr. Harris said as the girls loaded four boxes in the backseat. "You didn't give me a Leaning Tower of Pisa or a seven-foot-tall spinning sphere to build for you this week."

"Nope," Kylie said, climbing in beside the boxes. "No crazy cupcake display. This order was easy-peasy, lemon-squeezy."

"Every time you say that you jinx us," Sadie reminded her. "Remember when we had to deliver that order to the horse show and we got stuck in traffic for two hours?"

Her dad tuned to the news on the radio. "Traffic reporter says it's all clear," he said. "We should be there in plenty of time."

"You see?" Kylie said. "No need to worry, Sadie."

They made it to the party with a half hour to spare. The trampoline studio was a giant, indoor play-park, filled with ball pits, slides, tumbling mats, and—of course—trampolines of all shapes and sizes for kids to jump on.

"Where would you like us to put these?" Sadie asked the birthday boy's mom. She and Kylie each carried two boxes.

"Why don't you set them down over there?" The mom pointed to a table decorated with dinosaur plates, cups, and streamers. "We have some platters for you to arrange them on."

"*Roar!*" A little boy jumped out in front of Sadie. She was startled for a second—and nearly dropped the boxes of cupcakes.

"Hey!" she said, tightening her grip. "You scared me! We almost had a cupcake catastrophe."

"*ROAR!*" the boy repeated. "That's my T. rex voice."

"Well, it's impressive," Kylie complimented him. "You must be Justin, the birthday boy."

"How'd ya know?" he asked, eyes wide.

Kylie pointed to his T-shirt that read, "I'm the Birthday Boy."

"Oh." He grinned sheepishly. "I can't read yet." He

raced back to his classmates, who were all jumping head-first into a pit filled with colorful plastic balls.

Kylie glanced over at Sadie who was mesmerized watching the action. "You want to try it, don't ya?" Kylie teased her. "You want to go jump in the ball pit."

"Kinda." Sadie blushed. "Would that be silly? An eleven-year-old playing with kindergartners?"

Kylie put down her boxes and took Sadie's cupcakes from her. "I'll set these up. You go have some fun."

She put out all the cupcakes on the platters, admiring how each of the fondant figures attached to a toothpick was a little boy or girl in midair. They were perfection! She looked around the room for Sadie and spied her on a huge trampoline with Justin. When she walked over, she discovered the pair trying to outjump each other.

"Betcha can't do a knee drop into a backflip," the little boy dared Sadie.

"Oh yeah? Watch this!" Sadie expertly dropped to her knees, then sprang in the air into a flip.

"I can bounce higher than you," Justin taunted her. "I can bounce all the way to the moon!"

Sadie never backed down from a challenge. "But can you do it with your eyes closed?" she dared him back.

"Wait, Sadie," Kylie tried to warn her, "I'm not sure that's a good idea…"

But Sadie paid no attention—she was too determined to win this trampoline showdown. Kylie watched as her friend covered her eyes with her hands and bounced higher and higher on the trampoline.

"Go! Go! Higher! Higher!" Justin egged her on.

Sadie was laughing and bouncing wildly. "Check this out!" she said, doing another backward somersault—this time with her eyes closed. Kylie watched it unfold in slow motion: Sadie flipped in the air but missed the trampoline on her landing. She crashed to the floor and fell flat on her back.

"I win!" Justin cheered triumphantly.

Kylie raced to Sadie's side. She was lying on a mat, dazed. Her foot was twisted under her.

"Are you okay, Sadie?" Kylie asked, helping her sit up.

"Yeah, just embarrassed that I lost to a five-year-old."

A crowd of kids and parents was now gathered around them, and Mr. Harris pushed his way through.

"What happened, honey? Are you okay?" he asked anxiously.

"I'm fine, Dad," Sadie replied. "I just got the wind

knocked out of me, that's all." She leaned on Kylie and tried to stand up—but her foot gave way under her.

"Ouch!" She grimaced at the pain.

"You are *not* okay," Mr. Harris insisted. "I hope you didn't break something."

Sadie gritted her teeth and put pressure on her sore foot. "It's fine, it's fine. I just need to walk it off…"

She hobbled around the floor, and Kylie saw tears welling in Sadie's eyes. It hurt terribly.

"Sadie, I think you should go to the hospital and get it x-rayed," Kylie said softly.

Mr. Harris nodded. "I agree. I'll bring the car around, and we'll go to the emergency room."

Justin's mom brought over a chair. "I'm so sorry," she apologized.

"No, it's not your fault," Sadie insisted. "I was the one who told Justin I could do it with my eyes closed. It was silly and immature."

"It was cool!" Justin said. "But I didn't mean for you to get a boo-boo."

"I know you didn't." Sadie tried to smile. "Let's just hope it's not a big boo-boo."

R & R

If there was one thing Sadie hated, it was staying still—and that was precisely what the doctor at the hospital had prescribed. Lots of rest, lots of relaxation: fractures of the metatarsal bone only healed that way. She felt silly letting her mom fuss over her while she just lay there in bed with her foot wrapped tightly in a bandage. She'd skinned her knees dozens of times, even twisted her ankle and been on crutches. But this was the first time she'd ever broken a bone. Her pride hurt as much as her foot.

"I know you're not happy about this," her mom said, propping a pillow under Sadie's leg. "But it's Dr. Cohan's orders."

"Knock-knock!" her older brother Tyler said, tapping on her door. "So how'd you manage to break your foot? You didn't try some crazy trick on the new RipStik, did you?"

"I don't want to talk about it," Sadie grumped. Frankly, it was too humiliating!

"Your sister had a little accident," Mrs. Harris explained. "She was jumping on a trampoline at a birthday party and fell off."

Her other older brother, Corey, poked his head in the room. "Hey, Dad says you got your butt kicked by a kindergartner. Way to go!"

Sadie rolled her eyes. "Could everyone please just go away and leave me alone?" She pulled the cover over her head.

"What about your basketball game this week against the Stamford Sea Lions?" Tyler asked. He had a one-track mind and it was always on sports. "Coach Walsh is gonna have your head!"

"I don't wanna talk about it," Sadie repeated. Couldn't they just let it go? She knew Coach Walsh would be disappointed—the Sea Lions were a tough team with a near-perfect record. Then there was her cupcake club. They had so many orders scheduled and she was leaving them one baker short.

"This is a disaster!" Sadie moaned. "My life is ruined! Ruined!" She knew she was being a bit melodramatic, but that's the way she felt. Like everything that mattered to her had to go on hold because of this stupid accident.

"Okay, guys, let's leave your sister alone to rest." Her mom ushered Tyler and Corey out of the room. "I think she feels bad enough without you two making it worse."

"Exactly!" came a muffled voice from under the blankets.

When the door shut behind them, Sadie came out from hiding and reached for her cell phone to text Kylie.

Can't believe this!!!! she typed with a sad-face emoji after it.

You'll be okay! Kylie immediately texted back. Lexi's mom says broken bones heal quickly. She added four smiley faces after that.

Sadie sighed. Dr. Poole was a veterinarian. Maybe she was talking about dog and cat bones, not people's!

No school, no basketball, no RipStik, no cupcake club...what else was there in life?

Hello? Kylie texted. U there?

GTG, Sadie wrote back and turned off her phone. Nothing anybody could say would convince her this wasn't the worst thing that had ever happened. She wished she could hit Instant Replay and redo the whole morning. Why did she have to get on that silly trampoline anyway?

What was she trying to prove? That she was better at it than a five-year-old? It was silly and reckless, and now she regretted it. But it was too late. The damage was done.

Once again, there was a knock at her door.

"I thought I told you to bug off!" Sadie shouted angrily, figuring either Tyler or Corey had come back to torture her.

When the door creaked open, she hurled a foam football at it. "*Out! Get out!*"

Coach Walsh ducked, but the ball still bounced off her head. "Whoa! Take it easy. I come in peace," she teased.

"Oh my gosh! Coach, I'm so sorry! I thought you were one of my annoying brothers," Sadie apologized.

"Nope, just your annoying basketball coach," Coach Walsh said, handing Sadie a white paper bag. "I got you some jelly doughnuts. I always find they're the best medicine for whatever ails you."

Sadie nodded and took one out. The smell of sugar immediately perked her up. She was surprisingly hungry after the whole morning ordeal.

"I bet you didn't expect to see me here, huh?" her coach asked.

"Not really," Sadie replied, licking the powdered sugar off her fingertips. She'd never seen Coach Walsh outside a basketball court or locker room, and certainly never out of her green-and-white Blakely Bears uniform. She usually wore her black hair in a ponytail tucked under a baseball cap. But now it was long, loose, and flowing in soft waves down her back.

"Your parents called me and told me what happened," she explained.

Sadie rolled her eyes. "It's humiliating. I was at a birthday party for five-year-olds, and I fell off the trampoline because I was showing off."

Coach Walsh nodded. "I think you should stick to jump shots instead of jumping on trampolines."

"It's a pretty bad break," Sadie said, sighing. "The doctor thinks I might need surgery."

"I know. And I also know how upset you are—maybe even a little scared too?"

Sadie shrugged. "Yeah, I've never had an operation before. I keep picturing it like one of Kylie's Frankenstein movies."

Coach Walsh smiled. "I don't think Dr. Frankenstein will be doing the surgery. I'm sure you'll have an excellent orthopedist."

"I guess," Sadie said, sighing. "Still, it's scary."

"It *is* scary," her coach replied. "And sometimes you

have to face scary head-on. If a player from the opposing team is coming at you, do you turn and run—or do you stand your ground?"

Sadie knew Coach Walsh was trying to give her one of her famous pep talks—but it wasn't working. She still felt terrible. "Why did this have to happen?" she asked quietly.

"Things happen," Coach Walsh answered. "Stupid things. Bad things, and often to good people. The question you should be asking yourself isn't 'Why?' It's 'What am I going to do about it?' The challenges in life show us who we really are."

Sadie considered for a few minutes. "I guess I have to wait and see what the doctor says. She said we'll know in a day or two if I need surgery."

"Until then, you'll hope for the best, right?" her coach said. "No moping, no whining 'Woe is me,' no throwing footballs at people's heads."

Sadie chuckled. "Unless it's my brothers'."

Coach Walsh held out her hand to shake. "Deal!" Then she dug into the bag of doughnuts. "I could tell you 'doughnut' worry, everything will be okay," she said. "But that would be a pretty bad pun, don't you think?"

For the first time that entire day, Sadie smiled. "An

awful pun! As bad as one of Jenna's. But thanks for saying it."

"I mean it," Coach Walsh said, patting Sadie on the back. "The famous writer Oscar Wilde said, 'The optimist sees the doughnut; the pessimist the hole.'"

Sadie scratched her head. Who knew Coach Walsh was into reading—or that she could be so deep? She took another doughnut out of the bag and examined it. "You know jelly doughnuts have no holes."

Coach Walsh took a big bite. "Exactly why I love them."

☆ ☮ ☆

Sadie had to stay home from school and return with her mom to Dr. Cohan's office a few days later. The doctor looked concerned as she studied the new X-ray of Sadie's broken foot.

"I'm afraid it's not healing as I'd hoped," she informed them. "I think we should schedule Sadie's surgery for Friday."

"This Friday?" Sadie asked. "As in the day after tomorrow?" She shook her head in disbelief. "But I don't want an operation."

"No one does, honey," her mom said, trying to calm Sadie down. "But you're a very active girl who likes to play sports. You don't want your foot preventing you from doing that, right?"

Sadie zoned out as her mom discussed the details with Dr. Cohan—something about putting a metal pin in the bone to return it to its correct position, then wearing a cast for several weeks. She felt like this was all a nightmare!

"Thanks, Dr. Cohan. We'll see you Friday morning," Mrs. Harris said, helping Sadie down off the exam table.

All the way home in the car, Sadie stared straight ahead and didn't say a word.

"Honey, Dr. Cohan says she's done this surgery hundreds of times, and you'll be just fine. You can even go home the next day."

Sadie wasn't listening. She couldn't bear to think about it. She wasn't scared of most things—not bugs or snakes or horror movies. And people always assumed she was a tough tomboy or jock who never cried. But being in the hospital terrified her. When her cell phone rang, she hit Decline.

"I think that was Kylie," her mom said. "She said she would call at lunchtime to check up on you."

Sadie shrugged. She knew her friends were worrying about her, but she just didn't have the energy to talk about what was happening. She thought maybe if she never said the actual words, it would all just go away.

"I had surgery three times—to deliver you and both your brothers," her mom reminded her. "It wasn't fun, but it was worth it. Look what I got." She gave Sadie's hand a squeeze.

Sadie was sure her brothers would make fun of her for being such a baby. She could just hear them calling her "Fraidy Sadie" like they did when she was little. Tyler had his tonsils out when he was six, and Corey fell off a jungle gym and was in the hospital for two days with a concussion. Still, as much as she tried to reassure herself that this wasn't such a big deal, the fear kept creeping in.

"What are you scared of?" her mom asked softly.

"Everything," Sadie replied.

"That's an awful lot. Maybe you could pinpoint one or two things for me."

"Being on an operating table. It hurting really bad. Not being able to run as fast when my foot heals. Disgusting hospital food."

Her mom chuckled. "Yeah, the Jell-O is pretty lousy. But as for the other things, Dr. Cohan says the surgery is quick and painless, and your foot will be as good as new."

Again, Sadie shrugged. What if something went wrong? Didn't Coach Walsh say sometimes bad things happened?

"I wish I could be sure," she told her mom.

"On Friday afternoon, this will all be over and you won't believe how scared you were over nothing."

Sadie hoped that was the case, but wished it was already the weekend and this was behind her.

The Best Medicine

When Sadie woke up in her hospital room, her mom and dad were sitting at her bedside, smiling.

"You did it, honey." Her mom stroked her hair. "The surgery went perfectly and it's all over."

"Really?" Sadie asked, still groggy. "It's done?"

Her dad pulled back the blanket to show her a cast up to her knee. "You're gonna need to get a lot of autographs on this thing."

"Ugh," Sadie groaned. Her foot didn't hurt, but it felt heavy under the cast.

There was a knock at the door and the nurse poked her head in. "Are you up to seeing visitors?" she asked.

Sadie nodded. "I guess." She pushed a button, and the head of her bed rose so she could sit up.

"We came right over as soon as school got out," Kylie said. She was carrying a huge bouquet of roses. "These are for you."

"And these are from me." Delaney pushed in. She handed Sadie a collection of DVDs—all her favorite comedy movies, from *The Three Stooges* to *Despicable Me*. "Those little minion dudes crack me up."

"My present is the best," Jenna insisted. She handed Sadie a patchwork blanket she and her mom had sewn. In the middle was a patch made from a Blakely Bears team shirt. "To keep you snug as a bug in a rug while you recoup."

Lexi shuddered at the thought. "Eww, bugs in rugs? My present is much more creative." She unveiled a sketch she had drawn of Sadie flying through the air on her RipStik. "You can look at this and remind yourself you'll be back boarding in no time."

Sadie smiled. All of the gifts were kind and thoughtful. "Thanks, guys. These are great."

"Did we cheer you up?" Delaney asked, taking a seat on the edge of the bed.

"Definitely," Sadie said, handing her a Sharpie pen. "Do you wanna sign my cast?"

While the girls were all doodling on the white plaster, the nurse brought in a tray with a cup of green Jell-O and some sad-looking yellow soup. "Dinner is served," she said, setting it down in front of Sadie.

Sadie wrinkled her nose. "I'm not really hungry."

"Not even for your fave cupcakes?" Kylie asked, placing a box on the tray.

She opened the lid to reveal six perfectly decorated Mocha Toffee Fudge cupcakes. Each one was topped with an edible Blakely Bears logo.

"OMG, they're amazing," Sadie exclaimed. "You guys did this for me?"

Kylie smiled. "Of course we did. You're our MVP, Most Valuable Person."

"Do you have room for one more in here?" said a voice at the door. "It looks like a party." It was Coach Walsh. Sadie was relieved to see that her coach was still in her Blakely Bears sweatshirt and pants with a whistle dangling around her neck. She was carrying a basketball and placed it on the edge of the bed.

"Now, just because you're going to be laid up for a while doesn't mean I want my best player getting rusty."

"I'm sure we can mount a net on the back of your door at home so you can practice your free throws from bed," Mr. Harris assured her.

Jenna held up a cupcake. "And for starters, you can toss down one of these."

Sadie took a lick of frosting. Nothing had ever tasted so delicious.

☆ ☮ ☆

Over the next two weeks, Sadie felt like a princess, with everyone waiting on her hand and foot. Even her brothers were nice to her at first.

"That's a pretty impressive-looking cast," Tyler commented when she got home from the hospital. "Can I sign it?" Sadie handed him a blue Sharpie. "To my sis, Sadie, from your big bro Tyler 'Magic' Harris."

Sadie groaned. "Really? Magic Harris?"

"If the name fits…" Tyler teased. "You can be Air Harris if you want."

"I brought you some hot chocolate," Corey said, delivering a mug brimming with mini marshmallows to her room.

"Wow, I didn't know you knew how to boil water," Sadie said, taking a sip. She noticed the cocoa powder was in clumps, floating on top. "Next time, stir."

"I don't want you to get *too* spoiled," her mom said, bringing her a stack of textbooks. "Your teachers emailed your assignments so you can keep up."

"So much for time off." Sadie sighed. "I wasn't missing math and history."

Her mom opened to a chapter in *Intro to Pre-Algebra*. "Well, they were missing you!"

Getting around—even just downstairs to the dinner table—wasn't easy. Sadie had to hobble and hop down each stair, being super-careful not to put any weight on her bad foot. She held on to the banister with one hand and a crutch with the other.

Corey imitated her, hopping on one foot as he set the plates and silverware on the table.

"Very funny...*not*!" Sadie said, pulling a chair out to sit down. She was exhausted and panting from all that effort.

"Aww, come on," Corey teased. "It's a new dance craze—the Hop-a-Motion!" He waved his hands in the air and hopped in a circle. "Jump up...oh, jump back! Well, I think you got the knack, *Whoa-oh-oh*!"

Sadie put her hands over her ears. "Stop! Please! My foot hurts enough. I don't need a headache too."

Corey chuckled. "Ya gotta admit, you look kinda lame. Get it? Lame? As in you can't walk?"

Sadie groaned. So much for the royal treatment!

✩☮✩

The time flew by, and before Sadie knew it, she was back in Blakely's halls again—but this time she had an elevator pass. Carrying a heavy backpack around was hard enough, but with crutches and a heavy, bulky cast, it was impossible.

"Lucky," Kylie said, trying to make her feel better. "You get to ride to class in style! I've got theater arts on the fifth floor. Can I catch a ride up with you?"

Sadie pushed the up button. "Sure, you can be my assistant." She handed Kylie her backpack.

They rode up together and Kylie brought up the subject of the cupcake club.

"Speaking of assistance, do you think you're ready to get back to baking?" she asked. "Meeting in the teachers' lounge today after school. We really need you."

"Do you think I'm ready?" Sadie asked. "I mean, how much help can I be on these things?" She waved her crutches.

"Are you kidding me? Crutches or no crutches, you are a baking all-star."

"Okay…" Sadie hesitated. "I just don't want to slow you down."

"You won't," Kylie said, handing her back her bag. "See you at three fifteen—and you better have your apron on!"

Back to Business

Sadie perched herself on one kitchen stool and rested her cast on another.

"Well, look who's here! Welcome home!" said Herbie, PLC's new advisor. Juliette, their original advisor, had left her younger brother in charge when she got married and moved to London. Herbie tried hard, but he didn't *quite* get the whole cupcaking thing. He was more of a robotics-engineering guy—though he did have a sweet tooth and a good heart.

"Yeah, I'm back," Sadie said with a sigh. It felt strange to be in the Blakely teachers' lounge after so many weeks. She couldn't help feeling like an outsider. Hadn't the girls gotten along just fine without her? What could she possibly do to help them in this condition?

"First order of new business," Kylie said, calling the meeting to order. "I want to welcome back Sadie to the mix!"

Lexi and Jenna applauded enthusiastically. "And I'm sure Delaney will second that motion when she gets here," Kylie added.

"Did I just hear my name?" Delaney asked, racing through the door. Her school, Weber Day, was a few miles away from Blakely. "Sorry, my mom was late picking me up. What did I miss?"

"Just Sadie's return to cupcaking," Kylie said.

"Yay, Sadie!" Delaney cheered. "We missed you!"

"It's good to be back," Sadie replied, "but a little weird. What if I forgot how to do stuff? What if I mess up a recipe?"

"Only one way to find out." Kylie handed her a glass bowl and a carton of eggs. "Work your magic."

In seconds, Sadie had expertly cracked all twelve eggs with one hand without even breaking a sweat.

Jenna examined her handiwork. "Amazing. Not a single eggshell. *Chica*, you've still got it."

Sadie smiled. "So what's on the agenda for the weekend?"

Kylie held up an email on her phone. "How about a hula-rious cupcake order? It's for a surprise thirtieth birthday with a Hawaiian luau theme."

"Ooh! I can pipe those pretty Hawaiian flowers," Lexi

said, grabbing the phone out of Kylie's hand to read the details. "You know, white, pink, and yellow plumeria?"

"I think we should use a decorating tip and make green grass icing," Delaney suggested. "Like those grass skirts the hula girls wear?" She snatched Jenna's fringed scarf from around her neck and tied it around her waist.

"Aloha-oy! Aloha-oy!" She sang and swayed around the kitchen, waving her arms in the air.

"Aloha-oy...*dios mío!*" Jenna quipped. "You look like you're swatting mosquitoes!"

"I believe it's 'aloha oe,'" Herbie pointed out, arriving just in time to add his two cents. "It means 'farewell to thee' or 'hello' or 'love.'"

Sadie chuckled. She had missed her friends acting silly and Herbie being a know-it-all. The way they acted made every cupcake club meeting more than just business—it was fun.

"What if we sprinkled blue frosting with something that looked like sand?" she suggested. "Like crushed graham crackers."

"That's brilliant, Sadie!" Lexi exclaimed. "Why didn't I think of that?"

Jenna smacked her lips together. "The flavors could be very Hawaiian: pineapple, coconut, and passion fruit."

Kylie climbed up on a step stool and rummaged through the pantry shelves. "I know I saw some cans of crushed pineapple in here," she said. "We used it for that pineapple upside-down cupcake order a few weeks ago."

"Toss me down some shredded coconut while you're at it," Jenna said. "And some brown sugar and cream of coconut too. We can do a test batch on the pineapple coconut ones and pick up the rest of the ingredients tomorrow."

"Hey, Lanie—luau's over." Lexi snapped her fingers. "I need help making the frosting and filling the piping bags."

"Fine," Delaney said, taking off her makeshift hula skirt and handing it back to Jenna. "But I still think it would be awesome to go to a luau."

"Then why don't we?" Sadie suggested. "Why doesn't PLC deliver these cupcakes wearing authentic Hawaiian costumes?"

"My mom could sew them," Jenna volunteered. "*No problema.* I'm thinking some really loud Hawaiian print tops, silk flower leis, and grass skirts."

"Just make a skirt long enough to cover Sadie's cast," Delaney reminded her. "It kinda clashes with the rest of the outfit."

Sadie rolled her eyes. Delaney was always concerned about looking stylish!

"*No te preocupes*," Jenna insisted. "Not to worry."

Herbie held up his hand in protest. "Oh no! I draw the line at wearing a coconut-shell bikini top."

"You're off the hook, Herbie," Kylie assured him, trying not to crack up. "You can drive us to the country club where they're having the party, but we'll do the actual hula entrance and cupcake handoff."

"Phew!" Herbie mopped his brow with the back of his sleeve. "I'd be happy, however, to accompany you on the ukulele for your presentation."

Sadie rolled her eyes. "You play the ukulele? Seriously?"

"I've been known to dabble," Herbie answered.

"Sand...hula skirts...Hawaiian flavors...Herbie's ukulele..." Kylie jotted down a list. "Are we leaving anything out?"

"Hello? The big 3–0!" Lexi reminded her. "It's a thirtieth birthday party. How do we represent that?"

"We could use thirty ingredients in each cupcake!" Delaney piped up.

"And we could be up all night baking!" Jenna corrected her. "That's a whole lotta ingredients to pack in one tiny cupcake."

"What about arranging the cupcakes so they form the

numbers three and zero?" Sadie said. "I'm no math genius, but I think that's a simple solution."

"Sadie scores again!" Lexi patted her friend on the back. "That's perfect. We could build a wooden sandbox, fill it with our cookie crumb sand, and arrange the cupcakes to form a thirty in it."

"Then it's a plan," Kylie said, shutting the cover to her Peace, Love, and Cupcakes club binder. "And a pretty cool one at that!"

In the Dark

Jenna insisted the girls meet extra-early Saturday at Kylie's to try on their Hawaiian costumes.

"This is yours," she said, handing a light-pink floral crop top to Lexi. Each top had a matching grass skirt. "And this…" she announced, pulling a baby-blue shirt with dolphins on it and an extra-long skirt out of a bag, "is yours, Sadie."

"What about me?" Delaney asked, trying to sneak a peek in the other bag Jenna had brought with her.

"*Paciencia!*" Jenna said, playfully slapping Delaney's hand. She handed Kylie a bright-green top with palm trees on it and donned her own royal-blue shirt, dotted with the Hawaiian Islands.

"Last but not least," she said, pulling a bright-red halter top covered in sequined flowers out of her bag, "this is for Delaney!"

"Whoa!" Delaney said, holding it up for size. "This is so me!"

"That is so loud!" Lexi gasped, shielding her eyes. Even the grass skirt was made of red metallic fringe instead of the ordinary green.

"Like I said, it's so me!" Delaney squealed with delight. She threw her arms around Jenna. "Thank you, thank you!"

Jenna squirmed. "*De nada!* I thought you'd go loco for it."

"Are we ready to head out?" Herbie asked, inviting himself in to gather the girls and the cupcakes. "I've got my ukulele all tuned up."

"In a sec," Sadie said, placing her crutches under her arms. She watched as her friends each took a box of cupcakes. She felt useless.

"It's okay, Sadie." Kylie read her mind. "We got it."

"I know. I just wish I could pitch in more. I'm not used to being on the bench."

When they arrived at the party, the birthday girl's bestie, Bernadette, was in the party room shushing everyone and instructing them to duck under tables and behind chairs. The girls found a large table in the center of the room and arranged the cupcakes in the sandbox to form the numbers three and zero.

"Oh, these are amazing—and you guys even dressed the part!" Bernadette exclaimed.

"I choreographed an authentic Hawaiian hula for us to do for the birthday girl," Delaney bragged.

"Wow, that's what I call a special delivery," Bernadette replied. "Melanie will love it."

"Melanie will be here any minute," a guest said, waving her watch in Bernadette's face.

Bernadette flew into action. "Oh my gosh! Shut off the light! Hide! We don't want to ruin the surprise!"

The PLC girls did as they were told, scooting behind the long red velvet curtains in the party room. The room was now pitch-dark.

"I love a surprise!" Delaney said, barely able to contain her excitement.

"Here she comes!" another one of the friends whispered. "Everybody, on the count of three, yell 'surprise.' One... two...three..."

"SURPRISE!" the guests all shouted—but the lights didn't come on. Melanie couldn't see a single decoration or partygoer.

"Um, who's there?" she asked, confused.

"Someone get the light," called a voice from across the room.

"Don't you think I tried?" moaned Bernadette. "There's something wrong with it."

Sadie came out from behind the curtains and hobbled her way over to the center of the room, using her crutches to feel the way in front of her. She leaned on one crutch while she held the other one high above her head, trying to reach the light fixture hanging from the ceiling. She was tall, but the ceiling was nearly seven feet high.

"I've almost got it." She strained, trying to reach while keeping her balance. Finally, the rubber tip of her crutch tapped the fixture and the light flickered on.

"*Hooray!*" the crowd cheered.

Sadie smiled. For the first time in a long time, she felt useful.

"How did you know what to do?" Kylie asked her.

"It happens all the time with our basement light," Sadie explained. "The bulb sometimes gets a little loose and you have to jiggle it."

"Good show, Sadie," Herbie commended her. "You saved the day."

"No," Delaney corrected him before picking up a cupcake to hand out. "You saved our hula! Hit it, Herbie!"

Good as New

Dr. Cohan examined Sadie's X-ray one more time. "I think it's time we took that cast off," she said brightly.

"Today? You can take it off today?" Sadie's eyes lit up. She had waited patiently for nearly six weeks to hear those words.

"Of course, you'll have to go easy on your foot at first. No running down the court and no skateboarding till it gets stronger," the doctor told her. "And I'll want you to start physical therapy—"

"Anything!" Sadie cut her off. "Anything at all. Just as long as I can toss these crutches out the window!"

"How about you toss them in the closet instead," Dr. Cohan suggested. "Just in case you ever need them again."

"Oh no," Sadie vowed. "I learned my lesson! From now on, no crazy stunts that can land me in the hospital!"

Mrs. Harris smiled. "Can I get that in writing?"

☆ ☮ ☆

Sadie couldn't wait to go to the PLC meeting at Kylie's that night and show all her friends she was back.

"No more cast!" Kylie cheered as Sadie skipped into the living room. "I'm so happy for you!"

"That makes two of us," Sadie said. "I feel light as a feather."

"How long till you can play basketball?" Jenna asked. "Coach Walsh will be psyched."

"At least another month." Sadie sighed. "But it's so close, I can taste it!"

She decided she'd go to her coach's office the next morning and share her great news. She found Coach Walsh sitting at her desk, taking notes and studying her laptop screen.

"Hey, Coach!" Sadie called, then excitedly repeated everything the doctor had said. Coach Walsh didn't look up once from her work.

"Did you hear me? I can come back to the team in a few more weeks," Sadie said.

"I heard you," her coach replied, still staring down. "The Bears will be very happy to have you back."

Sadie couldn't believe her ears. Has she said or done something wrong? "But, aren't you happy to have me back?"

Coach Walsh sighed and put down her pen. "Sadie, there's something I need to tell you. I'm not going to be coaching the team for a while."

Sadie shook her head. "What? Why?" She couldn't imagine the Blakely Bears without Coach Walsh.

"I have to take a break," her coach said softly.

Sadie's heart did a flip-flop in her chest. "What do you mean *a break*? Why would you do that?"

"I'm going on a leave of absence for a while," her coach explained. "I haven't told any of your teammates yet, so please keep this between us until I do."

"But, Coach," Sadie said, "we need you!" She could feel tears stinging the corners of her eyes. What she really wanted to say was, "I need you!" When she'd been so scared of her surgery, her coach was the only one who knew how to help her through it.

"I don't want to leave," Coach Walsh said. "Believe me, it's the last thing I ever wanted. But I don't have a choice, Sadie."

Sadie tried to wrap her brain around what her coach was saying. Why wouldn't she have a choice to stay or go? Then she saw what her coach was jotting notes on—a cancer awareness website—and it came to her.

"You're sick, aren't you?" Sadie said, the tears now flowing freely down her cheeks. "Is that it?"

"Doughnut worry, okay?" Coach Walsh said, forcing a smile. "Remember what I told you about staying positive?"

That was easy to say when it was a broken bone. But Sadie could tell that her coach was putting on a brave face for her.

"Will you be alright?" Sadie asked her.

"I hope so."

"But you don't know for sure?"

"Sadie,"—Coach Walsh put a hand on her shoulder— "nothing in life is sure. And to be honest, I prefer it that way. If you knew you would win every basketball game, what would be the point of playing? Isn't not knowing part of what makes it exciting?"

"And scary," Sadie added.

"Yes, and sometimes scary. But like I told you once before, you have to face the fear head-on. I'm going to fight this. In the meantime, I'm trying to find a coach to replace me."

"No one could replace you," Sadie insisted. "That isn't possible."

"I appreciate that. But I still need to find someone fast."

✩ ☮ ✩

The entire day, Sadie couldn't shrug off the heavy feeling weighing her down. She had no idea how to help Coach Walsh—or if she even wanted Sadie's help. She couldn't bear the idea of her coach *not* getting better. And she'd promised to keep this a secret, as hard and painful as that was.

Kylie spotted Sadie at her locker and raced over to show her a crazy cupcake order that had just come in over email. "You won't believe this," she said. "This lady wants us to bake cupcakes for her pet rat! What flavor are we supposed to do? Stinky cheese? Garbage?"

Sadie was too distracted and upset to care. "Whatever," she said.

Kylie knew instantly something was up. Usually Sadie would have laughed and tossed out a few funny suggestions. "You okay, Sadie?" she asked gently. "I thought you were so happy about getting your cast off."

"I was. I am," Sadie replied.

"Well, you have a funny way of showing happy. You look like you just lost a friend."

"Don't say that!" Sadie snapped at her. "Mind your own beeswax!"

Kylie raised an eyebrow. "Sadie, what's wrong?"

"I have to go," Sadie said, pushing past her. "I'm late to class."

She knew Kylie meant well, but it hurt too much to think about losing Coach Walsh—for the rest of the season or forever.

That's What Friends Are For

Kylie wanted to call Sadie and talk things over—they'd never had a fight before or gone three days without speaking. But it was clear from the cold shoulder her bestie was giving her that she needed time to cool off.

"Why's Sadie late today?" Lexi asked, noticing the clock on the teacher's lounge wall.

"Beats me." Kylie covered for her. "She's probably so happy to be back at basketball practice she lost track of the time." She hoped the argument between them hadn't kept Sadie away.

"We have to be out of here by five," Herbie reminded them. "The custodial staff will have my head if we're not."

Kylie sighed. They did have a lot of business and baking to do. There were orders to discuss, cupcakes to taste test, even a new piping-bag tip to try out.

"I say we start baking without her, and she can jump in when she gets here," Jenna suggested. She held up a package of semisweet chocolate chips. "I'm starving and I'm about to break into the ingredients."

"Oh, no you don't," Lexi said, snatching the bag out of Jenna's hands. "Those chips are the spots on my ladybugs." She held up a sketch she'd drawn of a cupcake frosted red with black dots.

"Yeah, you can't make a lucky ladybug without spots," insisted Delaney. She studied the order sheet. "That's like a tiger without spots."

"You mean a leopard," Lexi corrected her. "Tigers have stripes."

"If Sadie doesn't get here soon, I'm going to start seeing spots," Jenna complained and pretended to swoon. "I'm so hungry, I feel faint."

"Give her five more minutes," Kylie insisted, handing Jenna a banana.

"This isn't as appealing as those Callebaut Belgian chocolate chips," Jenna said. "Get it? Banana? A-peel-ing?"

Kylie giggled. "I get it. And I'm sure Sadie has a perfectly good reason for running late." She glanced at the clock one more time. "I'll go look for her."

She figured the gym was her best bet, but when she peered inside, it appeared quiet, dark, and empty.

"That's weird," Kylie said to herself. "Sadie? You in here?" she called.

There was no answer, but Kylie thought she heard a noise—a drumming of sorts—coming from the far side of the gym. She walked in and found Sadie sitting on the bleachers, dribbling a ball at her feet.

"Hey," Kylie said, taking a seat next to her. "Did you forget we had a PLC meeting after school today?"

Sadie shook her head. "No, I didn't forget. I just didn't feel like going, that's all."

Kylie looked confused. Sometimes Sadie's basketball and baking schedules conflicted, but she was always a loyal teammate, both to the Blakely Bears and to PLC.

"You didn't feel like it? Why not?" Kylie asked. "Are you still mad at me? Honestly, I didn't mean to make you so angry."

Sadie stood up, tied her hoodie around her waist, and walked to the door. In the light shining in from the hallway, Kylie noticed that her eyes looked red and puffy.

"Sadie, were you crying?" she gasped. "What's wrong?" She'd never seen her friend so upset. Sadie was always the strong one.

"Let's go," Sadie said. "You're right. I shouldn't be blowing off our meeting."

"Never mind the meeting," Kylie said, grabbing Sadie's arm. "I'm your friend. Please, talk to me!"

Sadie took a deep breath. "If I tell you, you can't tell anyone, okay?" She knew she had told her coach she'd keep quiet, but she had to confide in someone! If there was one person she could trust, it was Kylie.

Kylie crossed her heart with her fingertips. "I promise."

"It's Coach Walsh," Sadie said. "I think she's really sick. She told me she has to take a leave of absence, and I noticed a site up on her laptop screen that was talking about cancer."

Kylie stood there, frozen, too shocked to say a word. Her heart was breaking for both Coach Walsh and Sadie.

"Are you sure?" she finally asked.

"Nothing in life is sure," Sadie answered. "Coach Walsh told me that. But yeah, I'm pretty sure."

"I think you should tell Lexi, Jenna, and Delaney. And Herbie! We have to figure out some way to help Coach Walsh."

Sadie took Kylie by the shoulders. "There is no helping, Kylie. There's nothing anyone can do. That's why I'm so upset. I feel like someone stole the ball out of my hands and won't give it back! I feel useless."

Kylie thought for a moment. "That's not true, Sadie. There's always something you can do. Think about how awful you were feeling after your accident and how Coach Walsh was there to cheer you on."

"You're saying I should be there for her?"

Kylie nodded. "Yes. And let us all be there for you."

They returned to the teachers' lounge and Sadie took a seat. "Coach Walsh asked me not to tell until she was ready, so I don't know if I should..." she began.

"Sadie, if there's something we can do to help," Herbie suggested. "I'm sure Coach wouldn't be mad at you for sharing it with us."

Sadie finally filled them in on everything she knew.

"Oh, poor Coach Walsh!" Delaney exclaimed. "It's so unfair!"

"She's really stressed out about finding a new coach for the team," Sadie told them.

"Well, I have a solution for that," Herbie said.

"You do? You know someone who could coach a girls' basketball team?" Sadie asked, hopefully.

"I do. Me."

Kylie had to cover her mouth to keep herself from laughing out loud. "You? You play basketball?" While their advisor was a whiz with robotics, she had never heard him discuss the score of a game or witnessed him shooting a hoop. In fact, she wasn't sure he even owned a pair of sneakers. Most of the time he wore shiny penny loafers.

"For your information, I was quite a cricket player in Canada."

"Cricket? You throw those chirpy little bugs around a court? That's mean!" Delaney protested.

"Cricket is an open-air game on a large grass field using balls, bats, and two wickets," Herbie explained. "It's quite a challenging sport, and I was an esteemed member of Cricket Canada."

"Yay for you," Jenna said, snickering. "And this helps Coach Walsh how?"

"I'm sure I could figure out the strategy for basketball," Herbie continued. "You play one sport, you can play 'em all."

"It's kinda like when you speak Spanish you can understand a little Italian," Delaney interjected. "When I went to Rome with my family two summers ago, my *español* totally came in handy."

"*Aye, dios mío,*" Jenna groaned. "*No es lo mismo!*"

"Yeah, what she said!" Delaney exclaimed, unaware that

Jenna had just said Spanish and Italian were two very different languages.

Sadie wasn't buying any of this. "Herbie, it's really nice of you to volunteer and all, but we need someone who can coach us against the New Canaan Coyotes in two weeks. They have an undefeated record, and they creamed us last year."

"At least give me the opportunity to do some research and present my case to Coach Walsh," Herbie insisted. "I'm sure I can convince her I'm the man for the job."

"It *would* be a great relief for Coach Walsh to know there was one less thing for her to worry about," Kylie reminded Sadie. "I say we give Herbie a shot."

"A jump shot!" he exclaimed. "See! I already know the lingo!"

"Fine." Sadie couldn't argue with all of them. But she suspected Coach Walsh would never go for it.

Herbie at the Helm

Sadie was worried Coach Walsh would be angry at her for betraying her confidence. But instead, she looked relieved. "I think it's a wonderful offer," she told Herbie. "If you want to coach the team, I'd be happy to hand over the reins to you."

Sadie's mouth was hanging open. "But Coach, you're not serious! Herbie knows nothing about basketball!"

"Nor did I when I started coaching," she said, handing him her playbook and clipboard. "Herbie will bring a breath of fresh air to the team—which is exactly what it needs right now."

"Thanks, Elisa," Herbie said, beaming. "It means a lot to me to know I have your vote of confidence."

"And it means a lot to me to know my girls are in good hands. I see what a wonderful job you've done with the cupcake club."

Sadie groaned. "This is never going to work."

"It *will* work," Coach Walsh insisted. "Because you are going to assist Herbie until you're back in uniform and can play again. For the next few weeks, I expect you to be Assistant Coach Harris."

"Really? I can help coach the team?"

"I'm counting on it," Coach Walsh replied. "And when I get out of the hospital, I expect a game trophy on my desk."

Sadie gulped. "You're going in the hospital? When? For how long?"

"I'll make sure that Coach Dubois has my schedule. You just worry about how the team is going to beat the New Canaan Coyotes. They're the only thing standing between us and competing in regionals."

"Coyotes, eh?" Herbie tried to joke. "That sounds like a howlin' good time."

Coach Walsh looked Sadie straight in the eyes. "Don't let me down. Remember everything I taught you. Make me proud."

☆ ☮ ☆

Herbie spent days preparing for his first coaching session with the Blakely Bears. He decided it was best to tackle the game of basketball like a complicated electrical circuit he was wiring in one of his inventions.

"Hey, team," he said, trying to sound authoritative and official. "I'm your new coach. You can call me Coach Dubois."

"You ever play basketball before?" Gaby, one of Sadie's teammates, asked, looking him over. He was dressed in a button-down plaid shirt, khaki slacks, and a red sweater vest. He looked more like an absent-minded professor than a coach.

"Oh, I'm quite the fan..." Herbie said. "Love those Red Sox!"

"They're a baseball team," Gaby corrected him.

"Right-o! I meant the Patriots."

"Football," Sadie said with a sigh.

"The Celtics are in the NBA," Gaby explained. "Ever hear of them?"

"Of course, of course." Herbie brushed it off. "I'm just such a big sports fan, sometimes I get all those teams confused."

Sadie rolled her eyes. This wasn't going well. She had to say something.

"Look, I know this isn't perfect," she began. "But you all know Coach Walsh is sick and needs us to pitch in while she's out." The team nodded. Coach had shared the news with them and the rest of the school earlier this week when she knew that Herbie was on board to fill in.

"Come on, it's not so bad." Herbie tried to lift their spirits. "I know I can't fill Coach Walsh's shoes, but at least I can mind the store in her absence."

Gaby scratched her head. "Store? What store?"

"It's a figure of speech," Herbie explained. "It means I'll be tending to all of you and your games until Coach is back on her feet."

Gaby shrugged. "I guess. If that's what Coach wants…"

"So, I've come up with a game plan for us," Herbie continued, checking his notes on the clipboard Coach Walsh had given him. He began drawing a diagram on the locker room chalkboard.

"Okay, if you go left and you go right, then that leaves this guy open here to advance the ball…" He mumbled to himself as he sketched a bunch of circles and lines.

"Um, first of all that 'guy' you're referring to is a girl— and she's a center. The other two are guards," Gaby corrected him.

"Didn't I say that?" Herbie tapped a piece of chalk on his chin. "It's called an early offense strategy. I read about it in my *B-Ball 101* book last night. Unless I'm confusing it with the Divide and Conquer?"

The team all looked baffled as Herbie continued sketching his plays. The chalkboard now looked like a tic-tac-toe board covered in scratches and scribbles. Sadie knew they had only a few days to prepare for the game against the Coyotes. And at this rate, they'd be running in circles!

☆ ☮ ☆

The day of the game, Herbie gathered his team around him once again in the locker room. "Let's go through the plan one more time," he said. At least he looked the part of a coach today. He was in a Blakely Bears T-shirt and jeans. But Sadie noticed he was frazzled and tired. His hair looked uncombed and there were big bags under his eyes.

"Did you get any sleep last night?" she whispered to him.

"Not a wink. I was going over everything again and again."

Sadie actually felt bad for him. "Don't worry, Herbie. You'll do just fine."

"I appreciate that, Sadie," he said. "Let's hope you're right."

He drew his diagram on the board. "Player 1 starts with the ball near the half-court line. Players 2–4 are lined up horizontally at the three-point line. Player 5 is near the basket behind Player 3. Player 1 passes to Player 2 on the right wing. Player 2 immediately passes to Player 3, in the middle, who then passes to Player 4 on the left wing…"

Gaby raised her hand. "I don't get it. Which one of those squiggly lines am I supposed to be?"

Sadie blew her whistle. "Listen up! All you need to remember is this: do your best. When we win today, it's for Coach Walsh."

Herbie stepped back from his board. "Yes, well, I think Assistant Coach Harris has summed it up nicely. Go out there and play hard, but also remember to have fun. Oh, and win!" He pumped his fist in the air and yelled, "*Hoo-hoo-hoo!*"

The team gathered their things and headed out of the locker room toward the court.

"Toes crossed," Herbie told Sadie.

"Don't you mean 'fingers crossed'?" she asked.

"No. We need more than fingers to win this game."

In the Zone

No matter many times the Blakely Bears tried to get the ball from the New Canaan Coyotes, one of the opposing players snatched it from them. By the end of the first quarter, the Bears were down 3–13.

Herbie called his team into a huddle. "Okay, I know this doesn't look good, which is why we need a strong comeback in the next go-round."

"Quarter. It's called a quarter," Sadie reminded him.

"Precisely! I want to pack the paint with our defense."

Gaby scratched her head. "Um, Coach. We're not really sure what to do. Those Coyotes block us everywhere we turn."

"The Coyotes have a really strong defense," Sadie reminded all of them. "But they're not as fast with the ball as we are. I think our best chance is to pass quickly and often."

"And they have good outside shooters," Herbie added. "So keep man-to-man pressure on them."

"You mean woman-to-woman," Sadie said.

"Yeah, that too. Don't give them a chance to shoot."

The second quarter felt like a whole new ball game. Gaby scored five points in the first few minutes.

"*Go! Go! Go!*" Herbie screamed from the sidelines, jumping up and down.

Sadie noticed that what he lacked in strategy, he made up for in enthusiasm.

By halftime, the Bears were back on a roll and leading 21–19.

"Okay, we got this!" Herbie said, gathering the girls around him. "Just stay on course."

But the Coyotes weren't about to give up so easily. They matched the Bears shot for shot, and with only a minute left in the game, the score was tied, 27–27.

Gaby got the ball but missed a three-pointer.

Herbie covered his eyes. "I can't look. I can't look!"

Sadie felt the same way, but forced herself to keep watching. Her eyes lit up when one of the Coyotes fouled, and Gaby took possession once again.

"She's got it! She's got the ball!" she said, shaking Herbie.

"*Shoot it! Shoot it!*" they both shouted. They watched as the ball sailed through the air and landed with a *swoosh* in the basket. The buzzer sounded and the Bears won by a single point.

"We did it! We did it!" Sadie and Herbie exclaimed.

The whole team danced around the court, cheering.

The Coyotes and their coach came over to congratulate them.

"Nice game," Coach Keren said, shaking Herbie's hand. "I guess we'll be seeing you at regionals. I thought for sure without Elisa, your team would tank. But you pulled it out. Nice job, Coach Dubois."

"No one is as good a coach as Coach Walsh." Sadie suddenly spoke up. "We owe her everything!"

"I'm sorry," the Coyotes' coach backpedaled. "I didn't mean it that way. I heard Coach Walsh is sick, and you're doing your best without her."

"She's fine," Sadie found herself shouting a little too loudly. "She'll be just *fine*."

Coach Keren looked at Herbie, concerned. "I certainly hope she will be," she said quietly. "I know it must be really hard on all of you making do and adjusting."

"You don't know!" Sadie tossed back. "And you shouldn't talk about things you don't know about!"

She ran to the empty locker room and slammed the door behind her. She felt so angry that she thought she would explode if she stayed on the court one more minute.

Herbie found her sitting on the floor in a corner, hugging her knees to her chest.

"Remind me not to get on your bad side," he said, taking a seat beside her. "You practically bit Coach Keren's head off."

"I'm sorry," Sadie said, sighing. "I just got so mad at how she was talking about Coach Walsh. Like we had to learn to get along without her. Like she wasn't coming back."

"Sadie, you have to understand that might be a possibility," Herbie said slowly. "Elisa doesn't know what the doctors will tell her. She's taking it day by day."

"But a lot of people get better," Sadie insisted.

"Yes, that's true. And there's more and more research being done every day to cure cancer."

"Well, it's not enough," Sadie protested. "Coach Walsh shouldn't have gotten it."

Herbie nodded. "I agree with you. She's a great person, and I feel bad that she has to go through this. But telling people off isn't going to solve anything."

"I know," Sadie admitted. "I let Kylie have it the other day too, when she was just trying to be nice."

"I heard," Herbie said. "But she's your friend, and she knew you didn't mean it. I'm not sure Coach Keren felt the same."

Sadie buried her head in her hands. "I just feel so helpless. Like there's nothing I can do to fix this. It makes me so angry!"

"I do have an idea," Herbie said. "Something I think will make you feel quite useful. I know what you can do that will help raise a lot of money to fight cancer."

Sadie looked up. "You do? What?"

Herbie smiled. "I have one word for you: cupcakes."

Cupcakes for a Cause

Sadie was excited to share Herbie's idea with her fellow PLC mates: a Cupcakes against Cancer bake sale! She knew they'd be as enthusiastic about it as she was. Focusing on a fund-raiser also took her mind off *not* being able to visit Coach Walsh and tell her about their victory against the Coyotes. Herbie said the coach had gone through surgery on Wednesday and was still recovering.

"She doesn't want you to see her just yet," he told Sadie gently. "Maybe when she's a little stronger. I promise, I'll text her tonight and see when we can visit, okay?"

Sadie nodded. She wasn't great at waiting for anything, but if that was what her coach wanted…

"We should do the fund-raiser as soon as possible," she said, circling a date on the calendar.

Kylie nodded. "I'll ask Principal Fontina if we can set

up tables in the school lobby. So parents and kids can buy cupcakes on their way in and out."

"And let's spread the word," Lexi added. "PLC is baking to beat cancer! I'll draw some posters."

"I'll ask Mr. Ludwig if we can also sell them at the Golden Spoon," Delaney added. "I'm sure he'd be happy to, and I can set up a display in the gourmet shop."

Jenna held up her hands signaling a time-out. "Flavors. We need flavors. Something that will wow everyone and sell, sell, sell."

Kylie looked in her binder. "Well, our most popular flavors are red velvet and chocolate-chocolate chip."

"That's fine, but we have to do Coach Walsh's personal fave," Sadie insisted. "Jelly doughnut."

Jenna frowned. "Doughnut? I thought we're baking cupcakes. Isn't that what we do? Did I miss the memo?"

Sadie tried to convince her. "But we need to find a way to make a cupcake that tastes like a jelly doughnut."

Delaney put an arm around Jenna. "You can do it, can't ya? There's never been a cupcake flavor that could stump Jenna *La Maravillosa*."

"Well, if you put it that way…" Jenna blushed.

"What do we want for decorations?" Lexi asked, taking

out her sketchbook. "Like a pink ribbon or something for cancer awareness?"

A lightbulb went off over Sadie's head. "No, not a ribbon. A gold trophy. I promised Coach Walsh I would bring her a trophy."

Lexi made a few scratches with her pencil. "A gold trophy molded in chocolate and sprinkled with luster dust." She showed the drawing to Sadie.

"It's perfect!" Sadie exclaimed. "Do you think it will be expensive to buy the mold?"

Sadie's mom couldn't help but overhear the commotion in her kitchen. "I talked it over with the other PLC parents, and we all want to pay for everything you need for this project," she told the girls. "So every penny of the money you make can go to the American Cancer Society."

Sadie hugged her mom. "Oh, that's amazing," she said. "Thank you!" It was the first time in a long time she'd felt so happy.

"Coach Walsh will love it," she told her friends. "I can't wait to bring her the check for the money we raise and a dozen jelly doughnut cupcakes."

Jenna was anxiously flipping through recipe books, searching for a way to make a doughnut-flavored cupcake. "*Por favor*, let me work," she said. "You guys start on the chocolate and red velvet and let Sadie and me figure this out."

Sadie took a jar of raspberry jelly out of the cupboard. "Try this for starters," she said. "I think we've also got grape and maybe strawberry."

Jenna made a face. "We are making these preserves for the filling from scratch," she insisted. "Nothing is too good for Coach Walsh's signature cupcake."

Sadie smiled. "You're right. This might be the most important cupcake we've ever made."

☆⊕☆

PLC had never worked so hard to make so many cupcakes in a week. "That makes 834 dozen, or 10,008 cupcakes," Sadie said, checking off a list as they stacked yet another box on the floor of her living room and kitchen. There were several dozen more in the freezer, waiting to be decorated.

"And at five dollars a cupcake…" she calculated. "That will bring in over fifty thousand dollars for cancer research."

"I thought you hated math," Lexi teased her.

"Math, yes. Money, no."

"Wow," Mr. Harris said, surveying the stock. "This is

a lot of cupcakes to transport. I think we should start with the ones going to the Golden Spoon."

"Aye, aye!" Delaney saluted him. She'd enlisted her school BFF, Sophie, to help her sell at the gourmet store after school. Jenna and her sisters would take the weekend shift. "Mr. Ludwig said he'll take two hundred dozen—and he'll donate all the money."

Tyler and Corey began carrying boxes out to Tyler's car. "We'll take this batch over to the high school and sell them there," he said.

"That's really nice of you," Sadie said. "I've never seen you volunteer for any cause before."

"That's 'cause this cause is about Coach Walsh—and she taught me everything I know about b-ball. I'll sell one thousand easy."

"Okay, that leaves us just 6,608 cupcakes to sell today and tomorrow at Blakely," Kylie said. "You think we can do it?"

"*Por supuesto*, of course," Jenna said. "Especially my amazing jelly doughnut cupcakes." She opened the lid of a box to let Sadie's brothers take a whiff.

"Is that powdered sugar I see?" Corey's eyes lit up.

"And wait till you taste the raspberry coulis filling," Sadie bragged.

"I don't know what *cool-ee* is but it sounds cool to me," Tyler replied.

"It's like a raspberry sauce you make from heating fresh raspberries and sugar," Jenna explained. "*Delicioso.*"

"Yum," Corey said. "Hand one over."

"Not so fast," Sadie said, slamming the lid shut. "That'll be five dollars, please. These are cupcakes for a cause."

Corey took a twenty-dollar bill out of his wallet. "I'll be eating at least two more on the drive over to school. Keep the change."

Tyler took a twenty-dollar bill out of his jeans pocket. "Here. I'll take one, and you can keep the rest of the money. Like I said, anything for Coach."

Sadie was touched. She hoped everyone who bought their cupcakes would be equally kind and generous. "Thanks," she said, handing her brothers a box. "You guys can have these all to yourself. Just sell the rest—we didn't make too many extras."

When they unloaded Sadie's dad's truck early in the morning at Blakely, Principal Fontina was already waiting.

"We've set up tables inside the rotunda and outside in the yard," she informed the girls. "And all the girls on the Blakely Bears basketball team volunteered to stand in front of the school's main doors and sell as well. I've also called the local press so we'll get people coming in and buying all day."

"This is amazing," Sadie said. "We're gonna sell a ton!"

"We should make an announcement over the loudspeaker," Principal Fontina continued. "Just as the parents and kids are arriving so they know what this is all about. Sadie, would you like to do the honors?"

Sadie's cheeks flushed. "Me? You want me to say something to all those people?"

"I think you could put it much more eloquently than I could," her principal replied. "Besides, you organized this entire bake sale. I think Blakely should understand how important it is."

"Go ahead, *chica*." Jenna gave her a little shove. "You can do it."

A few minutes later, as the crowds started pouring in, Sadie followed Principal Fontina into her office. She watched as the principal flipped a switch and a loud chime sounded.

"Good morning, girls and boys and parents. May I have your attention, please?"

She handed Sadie the microphone. "It's all yours."

Sadie took a deep breath. "Hi, um, this is Sadie Harris. I wanted to tell you about a really important fundraiser going on today and tomorrow. It's to benefit the American Cancer Society. I never knew anyone who had cancer before, but then someone really important to me got it. I hope you will buy a cupcake, or three or four, or a dozen from Peace, Love, and Cupcakes. We're baking to beat cancer!"

She handed the mic back to Principal Fontana. "Was that okay?"

"More than okay. It was wonderful."

The rest of the morning, the PLC girls took turns selling cupcakes in between their classes. Sadie had a second-period study hall, so she manned the second shift.

"The custodial staff would like five dozen, please," Mr. Mullivan said. He handed Sadie three hundred dollars. "We all chipped in. Please take this and tell Coach we're rooting for her."

When it was Lexi's turn to sell, the entire Blakely hip-hop squad—led by resident mean girl Meredith Mitchell—stopped by. "We want ten dozen," she said. "I don't really like cupcakes, but my daddy gave me this check to treat all the girls."

Lexi stared at the number written on it. "Does this say one thousand, five hundred dollars? Really? That's so nice of you, Meredith!"

Meredith smirked, "Well, of course it is." She noticed a photographer with a press pass snapping pictures. "Oh, here, get my good side!" she said, posing for the camera. "And make sure you spell my name right." Then she handed the boxes to her posse—Abby, Bella, and Emily—to carry as they trailed behind her.

During lunch, Jenna and Kylie were in charge. "We better sell a lot of cupcakes," Jenna complained. "It's chicken nugget day in the cafeteria, and I hate to miss my nuggets."

Ms. Shottland, Kylie's fourth-grade teacher, waved to them. She was leading an entire army of Blakely teachers, administrators, and aides down the hall.

"We came to buy cupcakes," she said smiling. "How many can you spare?"

"Are you kidding?" Kylie said. "As many you want!"

"How about we'll each take a dozen—and I think this should cover it." She handed Kylie an envelope, filled with cash and checks.

"That's five thousand dollars—we all chipped in," another one of her teachers, Ms. Levenharz, said.

"OMG, that's *más que suficiente!*" Jenna replied, counting the bills.

Dozens of students poured out of the cafeteria next, clutching cash and checks from their parents. A reporter from the *New Fairfield Daily News* was also there, diligently taking notes and interviewing students and teachers. "I'm going to write a story for tomorrow's paper," she told the girls. "Let's spread the word and get you even more customers."

"I can't believe this," Kylie said, handing out cupcake after cupcake. "I wonder if we'll make even more money than we planned."

Sadie could barely make it through the crowd to reach them. "This is amazing," she said. "I wish Coach Walsh could see how much support she has here at Blakely."

Herbie snuck up behind them. "Then I think you should go visit her and tell her. She's expecting us after school tomorrow."

☆ ☮ ☆

As promised, the *Daily News* ran a front-page story that was out Friday morning.

"Sadie, look. It's me!" Lexi said, waving the paper in

her face. There was a large photo of her handing a box of chocolate-chocolate chip cupcakes to Meredith Mitchell.

"Lemme see that," Jenna said, snatching it away. She skimmed the article, where Meredith was quoted as saying, "I did my part for this bake sale, because that's the kind of person I am."

"Ugh, Meredith." Kylie groaned. "She always has to be in the spotlight, doesn't she? Even if this sale had nothing to do with her."

"It's okay," Sadie assured them. "It's all good. Meredith or no Meredith, this is great publicity."

Kylie peeked out the window of the school's front doors. "OMG, they're already lining up outside."

This time, Ms. Fine, the PTA president, showed up with a group of parent volunteers.

"We'd like to help," she said. "You girls have worked so hard! We sent out a blast to all the Blakely parents and alumni, and we expect a huge rush this morning. We'll fill in for you."

"Thank you!" Sadie said, handing over the cash box. "I really can't miss first-period algebra or I'll be totally lost."

"Leave it to us," Ms. Fine assured her.

When Sadie checked back during fourth period, they had to replenish the cupcakes, and there was still a line out the door of Blakely, so long it wrapped around the corner. Ms. Fine was herding people through the doors and collecting donations.

"People have been amazingly generous," she told Sadie. "A lady who doesn't even have a child at Blakely handed me a check for two hundred fifty dollars! She read about the sale in the paper."

"Is this all we have left?" one of the parent volunteers shouted.

Sadie took a quick count of boxes and shouted back, "Thirty-eight dozen remaining!"

The crowd groaned in disappointment.

"But I need three dozen for my daughter's Girl Scout troop," said one anxious customer.

"I told my spin class I'd get us at least four dozen," another lady said.

Over the next two hours, almost every single cupcake sold, till there was only one box of twelve remaining.

"I have an idea of how to *really* make some money," Sadie said, standing on a chair so everyone could hear her. "Attention, please! We are auctioning off the last dozen cupcakes to one lucky bidder! It's a great cause, so please open your hearts and your wallets."

Ms. Fine followed her lead. "Let's start the bidding at two hundred dollars. Do I hear two hundred ten?"

"Two hundred fifty!" came a voice from the back of the line.

"Three hundred!" yelled another.

"Five hundred dollars!" said a man in a business suit. "My wife loves your cupcakes!"

"Six hundred! Seven hundred! Eight hundred!"

Ms. Fine and Sadie could barely control the crowd's excitement as the amount climbed higher and higher.

Finally, one voice boomed louder than the rest: *"One thousand, five hundred dollars!"* It was Principal Fontina.

"Do I hear any higher?" Ms. Fine asked. "Going once, going twice, *sold*! For a thousand, five hundred dollars to Principal Fontina!"

Sadie handed her the last box of cupcakes. "Thank you so much," she said. "That's a lot of money!"

"I was saving it for a rainy day," Principal Fontina admitted. "Maybe a spa weekend. But I thought this was probably a better way to spend it." She took a red velvet cupcake out of the box. "My favorite! This is the most expensive cupcake I've ever eaten—and it's worth every cent I paid."

☆ ☮ ☆

At the end of the day, the girls gathered in the teachers' lounge with Herbie to tally up all the money they'd earned.

"Don't forget we still have the Golden Spoon's weekend sales," Lexi reminded them. "But Delaney says she and Sophie have already made ten thousand dollars."

"Tyler texted me that his high school sold all one thousand cupcakes and made over seven thousand dollars," Sadie added.

Herbie jotted down the numbers and tallied them up. He held up the paper and showed Sadie. "I think that's a pretty impressive number to tell Coach Walsh, don't you?"

Sadie had been patient long enough. As much as she hated hospitals, she couldn't wait to get there. "Come on, Herbie," she said, pulling on his sleeve. "Let's go."

Back in the Game

When Sadie walked into the hospital room, she found Coach Walsh sitting up in bed watching the sports report on the local TV news. She was surrounded by bouquets of flowers, stuffed teddy bears, get-well cards, boxes of chocolates, and balloons—so many that she didn't even see Sadie and Herbie at the door. Sadie noticed she looked a little tired, and her hair was tucked under a bandanna. But her cheeks were rosy and her eyes lit up as soon as Herbie parted the sea of balloons and waved.

"Sadie! Herbie! I'm so glad to see you!" Coach Walsh said, smiling. "Please come in."

Sadie wanted to ask how she was, but she was too nervous. So Herbie said what she was thinking: "So, how's the patient doing?"

"Good," Coach Walsh said. Sadie studied her face to make sure she wasn't just trying to be brave. "Really good.

The doctors said we caught it early, and they got it all with the surgery. So I can go home tomorrow and I'll be back to work in a week."

"Really?" Sadie exclaimed. "You're coming back to Blakely?"

"Unless Herbie is prepared to fight me for it," Coach Walsh teased.

"Not a chance," Herbie said. "The job's all yours as soon as you want it. I was just keeping it warm for you."

Coach Walsh beamed. "I heard about the win over the Coyotes," she told Sadie. "Coach Keren called me and said one of my coaches was pretty tough on her."

Sadie blushed. "Yeah, that was me. I'm sorry. I guess she just rubbed me the wrong way."

"As long as you brought me my trophy," Coach Walsh reminded her.

"The trophy! I almost forgot!" She pulled a small gold cup out of her backpack. "From our win over the Coyotes."

"Next stop, the regional champs," her coach said. "I hope the team is ready to train hard."

"We are," Sadie insisted. "We've already started."

"I've got them on a tight schedule of drills," Herbie reported. "And I've come up with a new strategy. I call it the 'Dubois Dunk.'"

"Can't wait to see it," Coach Walsh said, winking at Sadie.

"I like how you've decorated the place." Herbie tugged on a balloon string.

"It's very cheery, but the food is awful," Coach Walsh replied. "If I never see another cup of yellow Jell-O, it will be too soon."

"We brought you something else," Sadie said, presenting her with a box of cupcakes.

Coach Walsh opened the lid. "Is this what I think it is?"

"No holes!" Sadie said.

"Wow," the coach replied, taking a big bite. "What do you call it? A cupnut? A doughcake?" She polished off the rest in just two bites.

"Jenna calls it *delicioso*," Sadie recalled.

"Well, that sums it up," Coach replied, licking the sugar off her fingers.

"And we have one more thing," Sadie said, pulling a check out of her pocket. "We held a fund-raiser at Blakely to beat cancer."

Coach nodded. "I saw it on the five o'clock news. Pretty impressive."

"So is this." Herbie gave Sadie a little push. "Show her how much we made."

Sadie handed her the check and watched eagerly as her coach's eyes grew wide. "Sixty-two thousand dollars? Sadie, this is amazing!"

"I know it's not millions, but it's something, right?" Sadie said. "It will help."

"Are you kidding?" Coach replied. "Every dollar counts when it comes to cancer research. I can't believe you did this."

"We did it for you," Sadie said. "And for everyone who is battling cancer. So many people who donated told us about family and friends who were sick."

"Well, you know I don't go down without a fight," Coach said, winking. "I'll beat this."

Sadie knew that if anyone could, it was Coach Walsh.

☆ ☮ ☆

The next two weeks flew by, and before she knew it, Sadie was back in her Blakely Bears basketball uniform, dribbling a ball down the court. Even better, Coach Walsh was back blowing her whistle and running the team ragged.

"*Rebound! Rebound!*" she shouted. "Sadie, when you see the shot, take it. No holding back!"

"Yes, Coach!" Sadie called back to her. She tossed the

ball but it missed the basket by several inches. She had to admit that she was still a little nervous being back in the game, afraid to injure her foot again. She kept second-guessing herself.

"Time-out!" Coach Walsh blew her whistle and summoned the girls to the bleachers for a pep talk.

"Now, I know you all beat the Coyotes and you think you have nothing to worry about," she said. "Well, that's ancient history. The teams you're going to face at regionals are even tougher. This is a whole new ball game, and there is no tiptoeing around the court or being lazy. Do I make myself clear?"

"*Clear!*" the team shouted in unison.

Sadie couldn't help but smile. It felt great to have her old tough-as-nails coach back, pushing them all to be stronger, smarter, better players.

"Okay, hit the locker room," Coach Walsh said, studying her clipboard. "Sadie, you hang back a few minutes."

Sadie gulped. Was Coach Walsh going to scold her for being so nervous on the court? For missing that shot? Was she going to tell her she wasn't ready to play?

"I have an email for you from Coach Keren," she said.

"You do?" This was even worse than being bawled out

for a bad practice. The Coyotes' coach was probably writing to tell her off for being so rude!

"She heard you had a little cupcake business," Coach Walsh teased. "And she wants you to bake something for her team to inspire them. I told her you'd be delighted."

"Cupcakes? She wants us to make her cupcakes?"

"And given how you treated her, they'd better be pretty darn good ones. You owe her." Coach handed her the email. "Like I always say, 'Make me proud.'"

☆ ☮ ☆

"Are you sure about this?" Kylie asked, reading the email. "You want to bake cupcakes for your archrivals?"

"I guess I do kinda owe it to Coach Keren," Sadie said. "I was really mean to her. And to you. I'm sorry, Kylie."

Kylie smiled. "It's okay, Sadie. I knew you didn't mean it."

"I didn't. I was just so angry and sad and scared and frustrated… I lost my temper."

"I do it all the time with my little brothers," Jenna piped up. "Like the time they colored on my bedroom wall with crayons and I exploded. My *madre* calls it '*la bomba*,' when I get that way—*BOOM!*"

"That's what it felt like," Sadie admitted. "All these feelings were just bubbling up inside me. I guess I exploded too."

"I never lose my cool," Delaney insisted. "I'm cool as a cucumber."

"Not true," Kylie reminded her. "You were a wreck when you found out you were going to be a big sister. Everyone loses her cool once in a while. It's a good thing we all have each other to clean up the mess." She handed Delaney a sponge. "Starting with the flour we spilled on the kitchen counter."

"I have a really good idea for the Coyotes' cupcake decorations," Lexi said. She'd been quiet until now, busily sketching in her notebook.

"Let me guess: coyotes!" Jenna teased her. "Big, furry ones."

"As if," Lexi sniffed. "That would be way too easy." She held up her sketch.

"So cool!" Delaney exclaimed.

"Cool as a cucumber?" Lexi asked her.

"Better!" Delaney replied. "They're gonna love it."

Peace Offering

When the cupcake club arrived at New Canaan Elementary School after school, Coach Keren was already waiting for them outside.

"I'm anxious to see what you made me," she told Sadie. "It better be good."

Sadie hopped out of her dad's truck. "Well, it's definitely as big as my mouth," she said, apologizing. "I hope you'll forgive me."

"Already done," Coach Keren said, offering her hand to shake. "We all have our bad days."

"You're gonna flip when you see this," Lexi told her. "We've never done anything like it before."

Mr. Harris opened up the back of the truck and helped the girls lift the display out. It was a huge sheet cake decorated to look like a basketball court, complete with a four-foot-tall basketball net in the center. On top of the cake were dozens of mini cupcakes, topped with basketballs modeled out of orange fondant.

"Wait till you taste them," Jenna said. "We call them Coyote Creamsicles. Orange cake with cream cheese frosting."

"Sounds amazing," Coach Keren said. "You can bring them in here."

When they reached the gym, Coach Keren held open the doors so Mr. Harris and the girls could carry the cake inside. It weighed a ton and took nearly all of them to carry it out of the truck and up the school steps. "We have lots of hungry basketball players waiting inside," the coach said. "Better not drop it."

When they put it down on a table, Sadie was shocked to see not just the Coyote team but her own Blakely Bears waiting on the bleachers. Coach Walsh was there too.

"Didn't think I'd let the Coyotes eat these awesome cupcakes all by themselves, did you?" she asked Sadie.

"I thought they were the enemy," Delaney whispered to Sadie. "Why are the Bears hanging out with the Coyotes?"

Herbie was also there, proudly wearing his Blakely Bears team jacket. "Did I mention that Coach Keren and her team would like to hire PLC to bake cupcakes for their own Bake to Beat Cancer fund-raiser?" he said.

"You would?" Sadie asked Coach Keren. "Really?"

"As many cupcakes as you can make, we'll sell," she said. "And we'll do everything we can to beat your record."

"Beat sixty-two thousand dollars? I'd like to see *that!*" Jenna said smirking.

"So would I," Sadie spoke up. "In fact, I'd love you to top it. The more money you raise, the better."

Coach Keren crossed her arms over her chest. "I do believe the Bears have just issued us a challenge," she said. "Ladies, are we up for it?"

"*Yes, Coach!*" the Coyotes shouted.

"Wow, they're really competitive," Kylie said.

"The Coyotes' coach has been very kind to me," Coach Walsh pointed out. "She emailed me all the time when I was in the hospital. Thank you, Rochelle."

"I lost a really good friend to cancer a few years ago," Coach Keren confided. "I understand how you were feeling, Sadie. Truly I do. It's okay to get mad."

"I was mad at the cancer, not at you," Sadie admitted.

"I hope you'll accept this as a peace offering," Coach

Walsh added. "Even though we're rivals on the court, it would be nice to be friends off the court."

"I think you mean a Peace, Love, and Cupcakes offering," Herbie joked.

Sadie held up a cupcake. "Who's hungry?" she asked, waving it in the air.

Both teams raised their hands. But she gave the cupcake to Coach Walsh. "You first," she said.

Coach Walsh popped the cupcake in her mouth and gobbled it up. "Now that's what I call a slam dunk!"

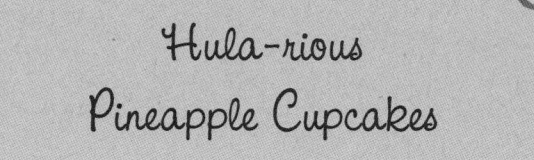

Hula-rious
Pineapple Cupcakes

Pineapple Cupcakes

Makes 18 cupcakes

- 2 cups all-purpose flour
- 2 teaspoons baking soda
- ½ teaspoon salt
- ¾ cup buttermilk
- ½ cup vegetable oil
- 3 eggs
- 1 teaspoon vanilla extract
- 1 ½ cups sugar
- 1 can (8 ounces) crushed pineapple, drained

Directions

1. Preheat the oven to 350°F. Line muffin pans (you'll need two to make 18 cupcakes) with pretty cupcake liners of your choice.

2. In a medium bowl, mix together the flour, baking soda, and salt.

3. In the large bowl of an electric mixer, mix together buttermilk, oil, eggs, and vanilla.

4. Stir in the sugar and pineapple.

5. With the mixer set on low speed, add the flour mixture; mix well.

6. Fill each cupcake liner two-thirds full with batter.

7. Bake for 20–25 minutes or until a toothpick inserted in the center of a cupcake comes out clean.

8. Allow cupcakes to cool completely, at least fifteen minutes, before frosting.

Pineapple Buttercream Frosting

½ cup (1 stick) unsalted butter

3 ¾ cups confectioners' sugar

6 tablespoons crushed pineapple, drained

1 to 2 tablespoons pineapple juice

Shredded coconut to garnish

Directions

1. In the bowl of an electric mixer, cream the butter until it is light and fluffy.

2. Add the sugar and crushed pineapple, starting on low speed and working up to high once the mixture is combined. The frosting should look creamy.

3. Add the pineapple juice and beat some more. You want the frosting to be soft and creamy enough to spread with a knife or flat spatula.

4. Frost your cupcakes with a knife or spatula. Top with some shredded coconut for that authentic Hawaiian luau taste!

Coach's Jelly Doughnut Cupcakes

Makes 18 cupcakes

- 2 ⅓ cups flour
- 2 teaspoons baking powder
- ½ teaspoon baking soda
- ½ teaspoon salt
- ½ cup (1 stick) unsalted butter (I prefer Plugrá)
- ½ cup sugar
- ½ cup light brown sugar
- 1 teaspoon vanilla
- 2 eggs
- 1 cup milk
- 1 cup raspberry preserves (My fave are from Sarabeth's!)
- ¼ cup confectioners' sugar

Directions

1. Preheat the oven to 350°F. Line muffin pans (you'll

need two to make 18 cupcakes) with cupcake liners of your choice.

2. In a medium bowl, mix together the flour, baking powder, baking soda, and salt.

3. In the large bowl of an electric mixer, beat the butter on medium speed for about a minute until it's light and fluffy. Add the sugar, brown sugar, and vanilla. Beat the mixture until it's combined, and scrape down the sides of the bowl.

4. On low speed, add the eggs one at a time, then add the flour mixture and milk, alternating between them.

5. Fill the muffin cups about two-thirds full, then use the back of a spoon to smooth out the batter. Since these cupcakes aren't frosted, you want a really nice flat top.

6. Bake for approximately 18–20 minutes, or until a toothpick inserted in the center of a cupcake comes out clean. Cool completely.

7. Fill a pastry bag fitted with a small, round tip with the raspberry preserves. Insert the tip into the top of each cupcake and squeeze some jelly inside. You know it's enough when a tiny bit pokes out on top. Sift the confectioners' sugar over the tops of the cupcakes and serve.

Coyote Creamsicle Cupcakes

Creamsicle Cupcakes

Makes 18 cupcakes

- 2 cups all-purpose flour
- ¼ teaspoon baking powder
- ¼ teaspoon baking soda
- ¼ teaspoon salt
- ½ cup unsalted butter, room temperature
- 1 cup sugar
- 1½ tablespoons orange zest, finely grated
- 2 eggs
- ¾ cup half-and-half
- ¼ cup orange juice
- 1½ teaspoons orange extract
- 1 teaspoon vanilla extract

Directions

1. Preheat the oven to 350°F. Line muffin pans (you'll

need two to make 18 cupcakes) with cupcake liners of your choice.

2. In a medium bowl, mix together the flour, baking powder, baking soda, and salt.

3. In the large bowl of an electric mixer, beat together at medium speed the butter, sugar, and orange zest until fluffy, about three minutes.

4. Mix in eggs one at time, beating well after each addition.

5. In a small bowl, mix together the half-and-half, juice, orange extract, and vanilla extract.

6. With the electric mixer on low speed, alternate adding the flour mixture and cream mixture until all are combined.

7. Fill the muffin cups about two-thirds full and bake for approximately 20–22 minutes, or until a toothpick inserted in the center of a cupcake comes out clean.

8. Allow the cupcakes to cool completely, about fifteen minutes, before frosting.

Cream Cheese Frosting

I like to fill the center of these cupcakes with frosting as well, to give each cupcake a real "Creamsicle" taste when you bite into it. Ask an adult to help you use an apple corer to remove a little cake from the center of your cupcake. Use a pastry bag with a large, round tip to fill the hole with frosting. You can then frost the top of your cupcake as well.

Makes two cups

> 8 ounces (1 package) cream cheese, softened at room
>   temperature
> ½ cup (1 stick) unsalted butter, cut into pieces, room
>   temperature
> 1 cup confectioners' sugar
> 1 teaspoon vanilla extract

Directions

1. Place cream cheese in the bowl of an electric mixer and mix to soften it.
2. Add the butter, and continue beating until smooth.
3. Next, add the sugar slowly on low speed, gradually turning up to high speed once it's combined. Add the vanilla. If you want to make the frosting more orange, add a few drops of orange food coloring (about 4 or 5 will give you a nice, bright color). Beat the mixture until smooth and creamy enough to pipe.

4. Using the piping bag, fill the inside of the cupcake with frosting. Then frost the top using the piping bag, a knife, or a flat spatula. If you want, garnish the frosted cupcake with a clementine or orange slice.

I was really impressed to hear about a young woman named Blakely Colvin who runs an organization called Cupcakes for Cancer (www.cupcakesforcancer.org). She was only thirteen in 2007 when she started this group to help a class-mate. Even more moving: Blake had been sick herself and undergone chemotherapy when she was only ten.

"I wanted to help his family, but most of all I thought if I could just put a smile on Kevin's face, it would be so awesome! I combined my love of cupcakes and my desire to make a difference."

I asked Blake to sit down and chat.

Carrie: When did you start your organization and why?

Blakely: When I was thirteen years old and in eighth grade I had heard of a boy in our hometown who was diagnosed with leukemia. I immediately knew that I had to contribute in some way to help him. I personally know the emotional and physical effects of chemotherapy after being terminally ill when I was about ten years old. I knew that hope could help restore faith to him and his family. So, I simply set up a cupcake booth at my elementary school with the help of all my best friends. The cupcakes were a dollar apiece and sold like hotcakes! And everything just took off from there.

Carrie: Tell us about your national campaign! Cupcake Angels and Fairies!

Blakely: Our national campaign is to help "frost hope across America." It allows anyone from anywhere to adopt Cupcakes for Cancer into their life and become an angel or fairy. They get to be in charge of their own cupcake sales, and all the profits go toward national cancer research. We have over twenty-five cupcake angels or fairies out of state and even one in Africa and one in Brazil!

Carrie: How has your mission evolved, especially now that you're not a teenager anymore?

Blakely: I have been able to take on more responsibilities without having to rely on my parents to help me out. Also, I have become very aware of health and how important it is to our lives...especially in preventing cancers and diseases. I am currently working on transforming Cupcakes for Cancer into a health promoter too, through the option of sugar-free cupcakes and various styles of more health-conscious cupcakes that still taste just as amazing!

Carrie: Who has helped you with your organization?

Blakely: My parents have been the most help. My mother especially since she was always the one driving my friends and me to the sales, helping with setting up, baking, cleaning up frosting messes, and helping with fees for the start of the nonprofit. My friends have always endured the long cupcake days with me when selling. It hasn't always been the most successful sales at times, but my friends always helped with their humor and sugary giggles to help me through. Also the community has been the best support. Without them, Cupcakes for Cancer would not be where it is today. They deserve just as much credit as I do.

Carrie: Since 2007, how much money have you raised and what does it go to?

Blakely: We have raised about $160,000 selling our one-dollar cupcakes! That is a lot of baking, if you can imagine! Every dirty kitchen mess was worth it though! We have been able to fund over ten wishes for the Make-A-Wish Foundation, provide for individual families coping with cancer, and donate over $25,000 to the Teddy Bear Cancer Foundation in Santa Barbara and national cancer research!

Carrie: Do you think that kids can make a difference in the fight against cancer?

Blakely: Absolutely! Raising funds to fight cancer can seem hopeless or overwhelming at times. But it is important to focus on what you are doing and what you can do. Even if the money raised is not significant, it is about what you bring to others around you. People are hugely impacted by charity work and a passionate effort to fight cancer. It will only feed their desire to help as well. You can spread hope so easily! That's the key to fighting cancer, in my opinion.

Remembering Elizabeth

This book was written for a very special person in our lives, Elizabeth Maria Walsh. She was Carrie's ballet teacher and favorite babysitter. We knew her from the time Carrie was in diapers. She was a ray of sunshine in everyone's life she touched. No matter how dark things got, she stayed positive and light. She was diagnosed in 2012 with Stage IV adrenal cortical cancer. It's one of the rarest forms of cancer—and Elizabeth was a rare individual.

She vowed to stay strong, fight it with everything she had and, above all, keep dancing. She started a foundation, Dancers with Cancer, to reach out to children in hospitals who were battling this deadly disease as well. Not for one moment was she sad or hopeless; she believed (just like Coach Walsh in this book) that you don't know how strong you are until strong is your only option.

She loved cupcakes, going to Broadway shows, tutus, toe shoes, and especially tickle wars. She was full of surprises—like showing up for a visit in NYC on a whim. She never let anyone feel sorry for her or pity her. In her mind, she was lucky. This cancer gave her an opportunity to reach out and help others. It gave her a voice to be heard. In fact, she told us how grateful she was for every single day—the bad ones as well as the good ones.

Elizabeth was an inspiration, not just for this particular Cupcake Club book, but to everyone who knew her. We hear her voice in our heads and our hearts every day. She died suddenly in 2014, after a fierce, courageous battle that included enduring numerous surgeries and treatments. She was unflinchingly brave and upbeat through it all. Her family and friends are continuing her charity to honor her memory. They welcome donations: dancerswithcancer.org/.

In Elizabeth's own words:

"I've said it once, but I'll say it again: I believe in miracles. Never give up on anybody, but more importantly, never give up on yourself. Miracles happen every day. In all you do, never lose hope."

Acknowledgments

Many thanks to:

The Kahns, Berks, and Saperstones, as always, for their love and support. Daddy and Maddie: love you to the moon and back!

Steve Walsh and Fatima Walsh-Espinal, Elizabeth Maria's wonderful parents. We hope seeing her words in print brings a smile to your faces. We love her so much!

Becky Keren, Carrie's Hebrew tutor and great friend who gets a shout-out in the form of Coach Keren! Besides your very own character, we owe you a dozen gluten-free cupcakes! xo

Dr. Beth Cohen at Uptown Pediatrics: you've always been our biggest cheerleader! Hope you like "Dr. Cohan" in this book! ;-)

Our super sweet agent, Katherine Latshaw, from Folio Lit; our great team at Sourcebooks Jabberwocky: Steve Geck, Kate Prosswimmer, Alex Yeadon, and Elizabeth Boyer.

All of our Cupcake Club fans who come to every signing, preorder our books, and race to bookstores the day the next book is out, and share their enthusiasm for the series with us! Hugs and sprinkles!

About the Authors

Sheryl Berk is the *New York Times* bestselling coauthor of *Soul Surfer*. An entertainment editor and journalist, she has written dozens of books with celebrities, including Britney Spears, Jenna Ushkowitz, and Zendaya. Her daughter, Carrie Berk, is a renowned cupcake connoisseur and blogger (www.facebook.com/ PLCCupcakeClub; www.carriescupcakecritique.shutterfly.com; Instagram @ plccupcakeclub) with over 105K followers at the tender young age of twelve! Carrie cooked up the idea for the Cupcake Club series while in second grade. To date, they have written seven books together (with many more in the works!). *Peace, Love, and Cupcakes* had its world premiere as a delicious new musical at New York City's Vital Theatre in 2014. The Berk ladies are also hard at work on a new series, Fashion Academy, due out on shelves Spring 2015. Stay tuned!

Check out
the Fashion Academy series
from Sheryl and Carrie Berk!

Big Dreams ★ ★

From the time she was old enough to hold her first pair of scissors in kindergarten, Mickey Williams knew she wanted to be a fashion designer. Way before she could even read, she and her mom pored over issues of *Vogue*, *Elle*, and *InStyle* together, tearing out pages of their favorite couture looks. Not many little girls knew who Coco Chanel was, but Mickey considered the fashion icon her idol and inspiration—not to mention Donatella Versace, Miuccia Prada, and Stella McCartney.

"What do you think?" she asked her mom. It was her sixth birthday, and she was giving one of her presents— Pink and Pretty Barbie—an extreme makeover.

She held up the doll that she'd wrapped head to toe in tinfoil and stickers. She'd braided its hair into an intricate updo and topped it off with a red-pen cap.

Her mom studied the outfit. She was always one hundred percent honest with her.

"I think it's a bit avant-garde," her mom replied. "A little edgy for Barbie. But that said...I like it. It's very Alexander McQueen."

Mickey nodded. "I was trying to dress her for a runway show in outer space."

"Aha," her mom replied thoughtfully. "Then I'd say that look fits the bill."

Mickey smiled. Her friends in first grade all thought she was crazy for chopping off her dolls' hair and coloring it with neon-green highlighter markers. They were grossed out when she replaced each doll's elegant evening gown with scraps of old clothing. But who wanted her Barbie to look like a clone of thousands of others on the toy store shelf? Mickey wanted all her dolls to be individuals in one-of-a-kind outfits. She could always find tons of fabric scraps at the Sunday flea market—all sorts of velvets, satins, plaids, and brocades in every color of the rainbow. For five dollars, she could take home a whole bag full! She and her mom loved hunting for treasures among the rows of cluttered booths.

"Do you like this?" her mom asked one Sunday as

they roamed through the stalls of treasures. She held up a brooch shaped like a peacock that was missing a few blue stones and attached it to the lapel of her denim jacket. "If you don't get too close, you don't even notice."

Mickey examined the pin with a critical eye. It made her mom's blue eyes pop, but it was kind of old-fashioned looking—what *Vogue* would call "so yesterday."

"Pass," she said, and picked up another pin—this one a dazzling emerald-green clover made of Swarovski crystals. "This looks so pretty with your red hair. And four-leaf clovers are lucky." It was only five dollars—a steal!

"I love it," her mom said, turning to the vendor. She hugged Mickey. "What would I do without you, Mickey Mouse?"

But Mickey's classmates were not quite as appreciative of her talents. In second grade, when she offered to give her friend Ally's doll a makeover, she never expected the little girl to burst into tears.

"You ruined my princess!" she wailed on a playdate. "I'm telling!"

Mickey examined her handiwork: Cinderella clearly needed a new look, so she'd given it to her. She combed her long blond hair out of its updo and gave it a swingy shoulder-length cut that resembled hers. Then she high-lighted it with an orange marker. Finally, she taped on a black felt miniskirt and a red, plaid strapless top.

"I think she looks pretty," she said, trying to stop Ally's bawling. "She could be on a magazine cover now."

Ally wasn't buying it. "I want my mommy!" she screamed, until Mickey's mom came running in and calmed her down with the promise of a glass of chocolate milk.

"Mickey, seriously?" her mom whispered to her. "Now I'm going to have to go buy Ally a new Cinderella doll—and I barely have enough money to pay the rent this month!"

Mickey felt awful. She knew how hard her mom worked behind the makeup counter at Wanamaker's Department Store—sometimes seven days a week, from opening till closing.

"I'll pay for it," Mickey promised her. "I have money saved up in my piggy bank that Aunt Olive gave me for my birthday."

Her mom shook her head. "Honey, I know you were just playing, but you have to use your head." She ruffled Mickey's blond curls. "If something doesn't belong to you, please don't give it a fashion makeover."

It wasn't the first time and it wouldn't be the last time

that Mickey got in trouble for "redesigning." In fourth-grade home ec class, the assignment was to sew a simple skirt to wear for the school's spring festival. Most girls chose a pretty pastel fabric: pink, baby blue, or lavender in tiny floral prints. Mickey's skirt was…different.

"Oh my!" Ms. Farrell gasped when Mickey walked into the classroom modeling it. She'd found a shiny brown python pleather and trimmed it with perfect tiny green stitches around the hemline.

"Is it supposed to be a witch's costume?" Ally asked.

"No, it's supposed to be Mother Nature," Mickey insisted. "It's earthy."

Ms. Farrell didn't know what to say. "It's…very…unique," she stammered. "Maybe we can put it up on display, and you can make another skirt that's less, well, dramatic."

But Mickey was determined. "No, I'm wearing the skirt I made. I'm not going to make one that looks like everyone else's."

So when they stood on the auditorium stage and sang, "A Tisket, A Tasket, I Made a May Basket," she stuck out like a sore thumb. It wasn't that she wanted to. It was simply that she had to be herself.

Peace and Love and CUPCAKES

Meet Kylie Carson.
She's a fourth grader with a big problem. How will she make friends at her new school? Should she tell her classmates she loves monster movies? Forget it. Play the part of a turnip in the school play? Disaster! Then Kylie comes up with a delicious idea: What if she starts a cupcake club?

Soon Kylie's club is spinning out tasty treats with the help of her fellow bakers and new friends. But when Meredith tries to sabotage the girls' big cupcake party, will it be the end of the cupcake club?

Book
1

Recipe For Trouble

Meet Lexi Poole.

To Lexi, a new school year means back to baking with her BFFs in the cupcake club. But the club president, Kylie, is mixing things up by inviting new members. And Lexi is in for a not-so-sweet surprise when she is cast in the school's production of *Romeo and Juliet*. If only she could be as confident onstage as she is in the kitchen. The icing on the cake: her secret crush is playing Romeo. Sounds like a recipe for trouble!

Can the girls' friendship stand the heat, or will the cupcake club go up in smoke?

Book

2

Winner Bakes All

$\mathcal{M}$eet Sadie.

When she's not mixing it up on the basketball court, she's mixing the perfect batter with her friends in the cupcake club. Sadie's definitely no stranger to competition, but the oven mitts are off when the club is chosen to appear on *Battle of the Bakers*, the ultimate cupcake competition on TV. If the girls want a taste of sweet victory, they'll have to beat the very best bakers. But the real battle happens off camera when the club's baking business starts losing money. Long recipe short, no money for icing and sprinkles means no cupcake club.

With the clock ticking and the cameras rolling, will the club and their cupcakes rise to the occasion?

Book
3

Icing on the Cake

Meet Jenna.

She's the cupcake club's official taste tester, but the past few weeks have not been so sweet. Her mom just got engaged to Leo—who Jenna is sure is not "The One"—and Peace, Love, and Cupcakes has to bake the wedding cake. Jenna is ready to throw in the towel, especially when she hears the wedding will be in Las Vegas on Easter weekend, one of the most important holidays for the club's business!

Can Jenna and her friends handle their busy orders—and the Elvis impersonators—or will they have a cupcake meltdown?

Book

4

Baby Cakes

Meet Delaney.

New cupcake club member Delaney is shocked to find out her mom is expecting twins! When her parents first tell her, the practical joker thinks they must be pulling her leg. For ten years she's had her parents—and her room—all to herself. She LIKED being an only child. But now she's going to be a big sis.

The girls of Peace, Love, and Cupcakes get together to bake cupcakes and discover Delaney is worried about what kind of a big sister she will be. She's never even babysat before! But her cupcake club friends rally to her side for a crash course in Big Sister 101.

Book

5

Royal Icing

$\mathcal{M}$eet Kylie.

As the founder and president of Peace, Love, and Cupcakes, Kylie's kept the club going through all kinds of sticky situations. But when PLC's advisor surprises the group with an impromptu trip to London, the rest of the group jumps on board—without even asking Kylie. All of sudden, Kylie's noticing the club doesn't need their president nearly as much as they used to. To top it off, the girls get an order for two thousand cupcakes from Lady Wakefield of Wilshire herself—to be presented in the shape of the London Bridge! Talk about a royal challenge...

Can Kylie figure out her place in the club in time to prevent their London Bridge—and PLC—from falling down?

Book
6

Sugar and Spice

Meet Lexi.

The girls of Peace, Love, and Cupcakes might be sugar and spice and everything nice, but the same can't be said for Meredith, whose favorite hobby is picking on Lexi. So when the PLC gets a cupcake order from the New England Shooting Starz—the beauty pageant Meredith is competing in—the girls have a genius idea: enter Lexi into the competition so she can show Meredith once and for all that she's no better than anyone else. Problem is, PLC has to make Lexi a pageant queen—and 1,000 cupcakes—all in a matter of weeks!

Have the girls of Peace, Love, and Cupcakes bitten off more than they can chew?

Book
7